To the Underwoods

First U.S. edition

Library of Congress Catalog Card Number 88-82330

10 9 8 7 6 5 4 3 2

First published in 1989 in Great Britain by
Walker Books Ltd., London

Joy Street Books are published
by Little, Brown and Company (Inc.)

Printed in Italy

Mrs. Goose's Baby

Charlotte Voake

Little, Brown and Company
Boston · Toronto · London

One day Mrs. Goose found an egg

and made a nest to put it in.

She sat on the egg

to keep it safe and warm.

Soon the egg started to crack open.

The little bird inside was
pecking at the shell.

Mrs. Goose's baby was very small.
She was fluffy and yellow.

Mrs. Goose took her baby out
to eat some grass.

But her baby didn't want to eat grass.
She ran off to look for
something different.

Mrs. Goose took her baby to the pond
to teach her how to swim.

But her baby just sat on the shore.

 Mrs. Goose's baby grew

and grew

and grew.

Mrs. Goose's feathers
were smooth and white.

Her baby's feathers were brown.
They weren't smooth at all.

Mrs. Goose had large webbed feet.
Her baby had little
pointy toes.

The baby followed Mrs. Goose everywhere
and cuddled up to her at night.

Mrs. Goose loved her baby very much and kept her safe from strangers.

Mrs. Goose's baby never did
eat much grass.

HONK!

She never did go swimming
in the pond.

And everyone except Mrs. Goose knew why.

Mrs. Goose's baby was a

CHICKEN!